Title: The Stars That Separate Us
Subtitle: Gay MM and Alien Shifter Romance Story

Copyright © 2022 by Jessie Perry (Author)

Thank you very much for purchasing this book.

Table of Contents

The Stars That Separate Us
Description

After Jared's parents pass away, things suddenly become tight. Jared finds himself in desperate need of cash if he wants to save the land he has grown up on from the bank, the government, and anyone who he owes debts to. However, he too is struggling with his own grief after losing his parents, and he can't seem to find the energy to get things moving. Things seem to be going down the toilet, and it isn't getting better. Then a meteor lands smack in the middle of his hard worked land. Jared rushes out to see what it is. And what he finds changes his life forever. As an alien crawls from the star that fell from the sky, Jared is left with a million questions: What is this? Who is this? Why is he here, and why is Jared so attracted to him?

Chapter 1

Jared loved his land, and he would do anything to protect it. There was no way to stop him from staying on his land. He'd handled his land for years, and it had been within his family since the day Jared was born. He'd worked as a ranch hand since he was old enough to walk, and wouldn't have it any other way. He loved working with the horses and the animals, chopping his own wood for his home in the winter, and preserving berries and jams from the fruits that came from his garden. He loved living off the land, and it had always been good to him.

That's why, as he stared at the bills on his table, he considered selling his left kidney.

Work hadn't been good lately for Jared, who was mainly a rancher and farmer. He spent his weeks planting, harvesting, and preserving things from his ranch. He sold meat, cheeses and everything else to vendors and more, which was usually steady income. However, for some reason, now no one wanted to purchase anything from him. There appeared to be a disconnection between him and the buyers.

The farmers' markets were slowly but certainly going away. Not enough people wanted farm to table foods anymore. Now, they could go to Wal-Mart, browse Amazon or anywhere else to see what they wanted. They didn't care about all the work Jared put into his land each and every day. They didn't care about any of it, and it was killing Jared. He was angry, sad, and most of all, it made him miss his dad, which made him feel lonelier.

His father had passed away three years ago. Jared had a void in his life and hole in his heart. It ached every time Jared thought about his father.

His father used to run the ranch. He was the head rancher, and his wife did all the gardening. Jared's mother and father struggled for years to conceive. When Jared arrived they taught him everything. His mother taught him how to bake and garden. His father taught him how to run a ranch. He was their only child and their little angel. When Jared knew he was gay, he didn't waste any time telling his parents. Jared was never one to hide who he was, and he didn't want to lie to them. They were his best friends, after all. When he told them, they listened and nodded their heads in acknowledgment. There was a moment where Jared's dad got up and left the room, and his mother cried a little bit. She was grieving for grandchildren that she would never get to have. Jared had to convince her that he had plans to adopt. When he did, and promised her that she would get her grandchildren, she suddenly changed the way she was looking at him. She wiped her nose, smiled, and told him, "Honey, I'm sorry. I don't care if I'm happy. You're the one who needs to be happy, baby. This is your life. Live it your way."

They hugged and Jared, who was seventeen at the time, went to bed thinking his father hated him. There was a separation between them, and his father had never come back inside after leaving. That next morning, his father didn't wake him up to do the morning chores. Jared had gone downstairs, scared to death. What he found made him cry on the floor with tears of joy.

His dad had a stack of books on the counter about parenting a gay child. He had gotten a shirt with the gay flag. His mother was making pancakes with a smirk. They still loved Jared, no matter who he loved in the future. His parents were really kind to him from that day on, and he and his father had a great hug when he had come in from a day of ranching.

When they had found out his father had cancer, Jared was floored. It was a stage four, terminal case. There wasn't anything they could do. They had caught it too late. They talked it over as a family and agreed that chemo wasn't worth since he had terminal cancer. He didn't want that radiation in his body, and he hated the idea of dying in the hospital and not on the land they had for generations.

It took about a year for him to die. Jared had opted to stay home instead of go to college. He took over for his dad and took trips with them for the rest of that year, making as many memories as possible. A few days before his father passed, he looked sickly. He looked like a shell of the man he once was, but Jared tried not to get into it too much. He had sat with his father, and his father pushed a paper over. He was too weak to talk, but on the paper he had scribbled, "I love you." He died a few days after that.

Jared decided then he wasn't going to go to college. He was going to major in history and become a teacher. Instead, he decided to stay with his mother and began ranching. His mother had stopped wanting to go outside, stopped wanting to move anywhere but from the bed she had shared with her husband. She hated seeing the house empty without her husband, who was truly her soulmate. Jared's parents had been best friends and high school sweethearts. Jared knew that when his father passed away, his mother would quickly pass away as well. Sure enough, she died from a broken heart a few weeks later.

Jared never knew that kind of love. Sure, he had some boyfriends in high school, but he never really found the right guy. They were either too pushy for sex, closeted, or not ready to date like Jared was. Most of the time they were just not a right fit for him. Jared hated that he wasn't able to settle down with someone before his mother passed. He knew that she would have been a wonderful grandmother, and he wished that there was so much more that he could have done for. He stayed to help them and never regretted it, but he had to admit to himself that seeing these bills made him wish that he had more time to go to college after all. He wished he had a stable job, one with a steady paycheck and benefits instead of stress and worry over the unpaid bills. At this rate, Jared would have to sell his land and pack it up. He would have to get into his truck and find a new place to live. However, without his land, his entire livelihood would be gone. He wouldn't have any way to make money. There would be no garden, no cattle, no land, nothing. He would be homeless and jobless if he didn't figure out something fast. He knew he needed to, but he had no idea what to do. Selling his blood or plasma flashed his mind, but he didn't have much more time to think about the bills and the stupidest things he could think of to pay for anything. He looked up, outside his big window in the front, and scowled.

There was something in the window.

It wasn't a creepy thing in the window, but it was still weird. There was no reason that the star should be that bright. It looked like a shooting star, but it was still way too bright. In fact, it was lighting up the entire night sky, which was a feat all on its own. Jared covered his eyes as if he were looking into the sun, and clenched his teeth. He looked to the side, covering his face, and then realized that the reason he was having to cover his face was because the light was somehow getting brighter.

"That's impossible," he whispered.

If it was getting brighter, it was heading toward him, whatever it was. The idea was insane. Why...how!? Why would something be coming straight for him like that? That would be impossible. Shooting stars don't tumble toward Earth. Maybe Jared was grief stricken. Maybe he shouldn't have missed that appointment with his therapist after all. Then his power went out.

Now this wasn't a joke. He jumped to his feet, panicking. If his power went out, then maybe...no. There was no way that whatever was coming toward him was anything but his mind playing tricks on him.

Unless it wasn't.

Jared jumped from his chair and grabbed his jacket from the hook and dashed out the door as he put it on. He looked up at the sky, frozen in fear. Sure enough, whatever it was appeared to be coming straight toward him. The orb of light was getting stronger and brighter the closer it got to Earth, and Jared was terrified.

What was it? A meteor crashing into Earth to destroy it? Was it a nuke sent by one of the countries that hated America, finally getting pissed enough to launch something and send the world into an all-out war? Was it a star, coming to destroy Earth? Was it kind of a Superman situation, and Jared would find himself stuck with a super child to raise to fight evil? Or would it be God sending him a giant pile of money, trying to make up for all the shit he put Jared through?

His cows mooed and cried out, kicking out their feet and begging Jared to turn off whatever big flashlight he was shining at them. Jared watched the light as long as he could, following the trajectory with his index finger and trying to decipher where it was going to land.

His heart stopped when he realized it was going to crash land somewhere in his ranch.

Jared panicked. He took off toward where the light was going to go, trying to get there before the thing from the sky reached it. He ran as fast as he could, tripping twice over his own feet. He wasn't sure why he was running, he knew better than to do that, in fact. There was no way he was going to be able to beat the meteor or whatever it was. He knew that even if he were to be it, what was he going to do? Stop it with his bare hands?

Still, he kept running. Maybe if he were to make it there before the light, he would be able to stop it from hurting someone or any of his animals. If something was in the way, he could move it.

For a minute, Jared fantasized what it would be like for it to be a meteor. What would he do if it was a giant space rock made of something like gold? Something that he could sell to save the farm? What if whatever was crashing toward his land was some twisted answer to his prayers?

Or, on the flip side, what if the thing coming to the Earth was some kind of space monster and Jared would be his first victim? Either way, Jared's problems would be solved.

Jared wanted to mentally slap himself for that comment. He knew better than to joke about that. That was wrong.

When the big bright light of whatever did come crashing down to earth, there was a moment where nothing happened. It hit the ground like it was nothing, like it was air. Jared stopped running, kind of staggering backward with wide eyes. Why hadn't the crashing thing made a sound? Why wasn't it moving or making some kind of call?

Then it came crashing down.

Chapter 2

The soundwave that rippled from the thing that came to his planet was so loud Jared barely had time to cover his ears. He screamed and fell to his knees, praying that it would end soon. Luckily, it did, but the wave traveled as waves do. He heard his car windows shatter and his alarm go off, blaring. He heard the trees woosh angrily in protest to the wave. He heard a shriek from the cows and foals, the bleating protests from the goats as they probably tried to eat the waves. The windows in his home, made of glass of course, also shattered. Jared cursed, but he couldn't even hear himself.

Next came the dirt.

Jared didn't even think about the dirt. He watched what looked like a storm of soil heading his way, super-fast and unforgiving. Jared only had time to fall to the ground and cover his head with his arms before the dirt was on him.

He buried his head in the shield that his arms and forearms provided him, covering his ears with his hands. He didn't want dirt getting into his nose and mouth since that would not only be a health hazard but a nuisance. He screamed against the oncoming dirt, knowing that it would probably make him feel better to do so. In a way, it did. It helped him feel like he was screaming at everything in his life that had gone wrong for him. It made him feel like he was screaming at cancer for taking his parents, at money for taking his land, and at the world for taking his soul.

Of course, it didn't do any good against the torrenting winds.

Jared continued screaming in anger, but it also turned into screams of anguish. His bare hands were being picked to shreds by the rocks and pieces of dirt, slicing his hands to shreds. Jared even felt his forearms begin to tear as his flimsy jacket was ripped. He wondered when the dirt would stop, feeling like he was in a desert sandstorm. God, he just wanted it to stop. Hadn't he dealt with enough in his life already? Why did he have to deal with this?

Then, suddenly, it stopped.

Jared didn't move for a while. He was afraid that if he did, he would somehow jinx whatever balance was going on right now that calmed everything down, so instead, he just sat and listened. He heard the dirt settle with a defiant woosh. He heard the sound of the cattle mooing and the goats crying out, all of them also probably just as scared as Jared was. There were no movements, no dirt, no nothing. Jared, and Jared decided it was time to move.

He slowly lifted his head from his arms and peeked forward. One eye first, then the other. They peered out from underneath his arms, and Jared finally got to see whatever it was that crashed on his land.

He could not believe his luck. What looked to be a rock of pure gold sat near the big oak tree on his land, and of course the tree hadn't fallen during the crash. Jared could tell it was made of pure gold from the way it glistened in the moonlight. Even it weren't gold, Jared wondered if he could get away with pawning it. He couldn't stop the little whoop of excitement that escaped his mouth when he looked more and more at this thing, thinking about his future. Maybe God had sent him this as a reward after all. A little "I'm sorry" present for taking away everything he loved. Maybe all hope wasn't lost after all.

Jared clapped his hands together and rushed toward the thing. Surely he could call it a meteor now or something, right? It was only fair. He walked closer toward it and paused, suddenly hesitant. What if it was radioactive? What if it gave him superpowers, or worse, just killed him? After all, what was a giant chunk of gold doing up in outer space?

Jared didn't know much about outer space, but he was pretty sure gold wasn't native there. He took a couple steps back, contemplating what to do, and that's when the meteor opened.

"HOLY GOOD SHIT!" Jared screamed.

He was trying to say 'holy good God' and "holy shit' at the same time, producing that glorious amalgamation of words. The meteor continued to open up, smoke pouring out of it like some cheesy movie or Broadway prop. Jared wondered what the hell it could mean, but he was more focused on the fact that the doors were opening than the fact smoke was pouring from it.

If the meteor was opening, then that meant it wasn't a meteor. That must have been a ship or a door or some kind of portal. Jared fell onto the ground and scrambled backward, kicking up dirt with his feet and using his arms to propel himself backward. He was trying to get as far away from this thing as he could, and yet...well, he just wasn't sure anymore. Did he need to run? Maybe. Was he running? No.

Jared had no idea why. He really didn't know what he was doing, and he couldn't explain it, but he was drawn to the meteor. He wondered if it was some kind of weird magic spell the rock from space was casting on him.

That's when he saw what was inside.

To describe it as human would be incorrect, of course. It was climbing out of something from space, so obviously Jared couldn't say it was human. However, the being that crawled out from the meteor looked human. It looked so human, in fact, that Jared couldn't help but notice all of its...anatomy. The only way Jared was certain that this "thing" that crawled out from the meteor was an alien of some sort and not a human was the neon blue eyes, surveying the land. He sniffed the air, then looked back at his meteor.

He didn't speak or say anything, and Jared really wasn't sure what to make of that. Should he help the thing? Should he ask what it needed? Should he press it further, demand to know what it was doing here? Should he let him borrow some pants, if it even had a gender? Jared wasn't sure what to say or comment on, what to do, and then it suddenly spoke.

"Help," was all that it was able to say or do. A simple, "Help."

Jared's jaw nearly hit the floor. Whatever this thing was, it knew English. It looked human, and yet it came from space. What was it doing here? What did it want? Was this some kind of trick? Jared felt frozen in place, unsure of what to do. Finally, he swallowed his fear and spoke up.

"Who...who are you," Jared murmured against the wind.

Jared's car alarm, which was still blaring in the background, seemed to annoy more than just Jared. The being that stepped out from the meteor flicked their hand out toward Jared's car. To Jared's surprise, the car alarm ceased immediately. Jared felt his mouth drop, his mind stiffen. What the hell was this thing? An escaped X-Men?

The thing stared at Jared with what seemed to be a morbid curiosity. He was studying Jared, and Jared knew this. It was obvious in the way that he was looking at Jared. The creature's movements were jerky, strong. When he looked at Jared, he looked at him like he was something to eat. This did not calm Jared's nerves.

"Are you here to kill me?" Jared whispered.

The creature frowned. "No."

Jared was not put at ease.

"I am here to...walk among you. That is my job."

"Job?" Jared asked, but it came out more like a squeak.

"Yes," was all that was said. The creature didn't seem to find the need to elaborate further on the subject.

"I'm sorry but who are you!?" Jared demanded. "What is going on!? You just crashed down here on my land without warning me! You didn't even... you broke all the windows to my home! Everything is destroyed! You're going to need to replace that...somehow."

The creature looked at Jared's home. Then he looked at the field. His eyes were piercing as he gazed about, looking at everything Jared owned with a prying gaze.

"I am sorry about that," He offered finally. "I did not mean to disturb your living space. I truly ask for your forgiveness in this time."

Jared raised his eyebrows. "How do you speak such good English? You're from space."

"Maybe it's best that we talk inside," The alien creature suggested, gesturing into Jared's home.

Jared was about to follow him inside when lights appeared. It looked to Jared like five or six cars driving down the road, heading straight toward his house. Immediately, he felt a strong and sudden urge to protect his alien friend? No. Acquaintance? No. Thing? Sure.

"Get inside," Jared ushered him, but the creature didn't move.

"No," he said flatly. "I do not need to."

Jared shrugged out of his coat, flinging it to the alien creature. "Then at least...cover yourself."

The alien studied Jared. "Is this not acceptable here? You seemed to like it."

Jared wished he could die right in that moment. Oh, how he wanted to die.

"I...just...put the damn coat on."

"Do you want it to cover my penis or not?"

"YES!"

The cars came to an abrupt stop outside of Jared's home. Several men in suits climbed out of the black cars, SUVs and trucks. They all glared at Jared as if he were the one who had done something wrong, like it was his fault that the alien decided to crash to this planet and chose his plot of land.

"Jared Jones?" a manly voice barked. "Are you here?"

"Present," Jared mumbled before wanting to smack himself in the face. Obviously he didn't need to say present. Then again, he didn't really know what the protocol was for strange, obviously working for the government men showing up at your door.

"We have reason to believe a foreign object has crashed here on your land," one of the men explained. "We saw it on our radars, and I can see the vessel with my own eyes. We will need to take the subject in for questioning."

Jared didn't know what to do. He didn't trust the government as far as he could throw his own house, but he couldn't tell them no. It wasn't like he was going to look the government dead in the eye and tell them to screw off. He was sure he looked like a student that had no idea what was going on in class as he looked back and forth between the alien and the men in black, respectively.

"I don't want to go with you," the alien stated.

"Oh good God," Jared whispered.

The men in black raised their weapons and aimed them at the alien, who didn't seem shocked or afraid by the motion at all. In fact, he seemed to find it mildly funny.

"I am not going anywhere that I don't want to," the alien said. "You cannot force me."

"I do believe we can," one of the men barked.

"Isn't that illegal?" Jared piped up, but was ignored.

"You are a foreign entity on our soil," the main man in black barked. "You will come with us."

It didn't take a detective to figure out that the alien wasn't going anywhere that he didn't want to go. Jared wasn't sure whether to stop him or help him. After all, Jared felt sympathy for the alien that was going to be forced to go anywhere against his will. Really, Jared would sympathize with anyone who had this problem, alien or not. If he didn't want to go with the government, he shouldn't have had to. It was really just that simple, at least logically. Logically speaking, Jared would be able to kindly tell the government to leave. He would be able to tell them to get the hell off of his property and they would nod and walk away.

However, Jared wasn't stupid. He knew better than that. He knew that any kind of attempt to tell the government to "fuck off" would be met with serious resistance, and was he really willing to risk it all for some alien whot just walked off onto the planet who, in fact, said that he didn't want to eat Jared but wasn't very convincing.

"You haven't given me the chance to explain why I am here," the alien offered with a serious expression. "Why aren't you letting me explain myself?"

"There's nothing to explain," the main man in black demanded. "You are here on our planet. You will answer our questions."

"We do not treat visitors on our planet as rude as you treat me," the alien stated matter of factly. "You Earth people are very rude."

Jared wasn't going to argue with the alien. He knew he was right.

He also still wasn't sure what to do or say about the government being there.

"Um," he finally coughed out. "Um, can I get you guys some water or anything?"

The government ignored him again.

"Listen alien," the main man barked, "Either surrender now or face the consequences!"

The alien scoffed. "I'd rather take your excuse for a consequence over blind obedience any day."

Jared had to admit that he was floored by the raw line that the alien called out.

The government took this as an excuse and, since this is America, started firing.

Jared screamed and ran to hide behind a tree, ducking from the gunfire. He had been shooting with his father before, sure, but it had been hunting. Rifle shooting, and to animals that were in season. Not toward people, and definitely not pistols or anything else. There was no reason that Jared would be prepared for something like that, and yet in the back of his mind, he felt that he should have been. It was a weird sensation to experience.

He looked out from around the tree, watching the firefight. The government had been firing their weapons for a time now at one target, so Jared had to admit he was a little surprised that they hadn't hit the alien yet. He peeked over and noticed that the alien was literally taking in the bullets, as if they were little bits of a vitamin and gave him the energy he needed to exist or something.

He was completely shocked. He had never seen anything like this, unless it was in a movie.

"Maybe I'm in a movie," Jared whispered to himself over the gunfire. "Maybe this is just a prank or something, maybe it's immersive theater. Maybe I'm in a dream. Maybe I'm in a very serious, very vivid, dream."

Sure, that was the thing that made the most sense, but it wasn't explaining the way that the alien made Jared feel. When he looked at the alien, he felt that he had found something that he had been searching for...something he had been reaching for...for a long time. He couldn't explain it. The alien was attractive in a human sense, having muscles in all the right places and a very attractive penis, despite Jared's flustering at the alien bringing it up. Still, Jared had felt a certain connection with the alien when they had locked eyes. It was hard to explain, but it wasn't like anything he had felt with any of his previous boyfriends. He felt stupid even thinking it. He hadn't even had a conversation with this alien that wasn't more than a few sentences. How on earth did he think that he had some kind of connection with him? He was just a creature from another planet, of all things.

And yet, Jared couldn't argue with it. He knew he had the connection. He knew it was there.

His stomach lurched as he continued watching what was going on. The alien seemed to swallow the bullets like they were candy, grinning at the men that fired at him. The sounds of clicks, unmistakable gun jamming noises, filled the air.

The alien leveled his gaze at the men. "That was...cute. I'll give you that."

The men in black suits panicked. For a moment, Jared wondered if they were going to whip out a bazooka or something, or worse, some kind of chemical bomb. Instead, they reached for some kind of walkie talkie and...Then they stopped.

The alien was smirking, and his eyes were glowing blue. Jared watched as he noticed that literally every single man in the black suits was frozen stiff. Their eyes still moved about, independent from their body. The alien had frozen them stiff? Maybe? It was hard to argue with that as the alien walked forward.

"Now that I have your attention," he said, "Would you like to know what I'm doing here? Or are you going to be rude again?"

Jared stifled a laugh.

"As I said, I'm not going anywhere with you people. I have a job to do here on this plot of land. The man who owns this land, Jared, needs my help."

Jared's ears perked up, almost as if he was a cat.

"I'm sorry, what!?"

"The minute I touched the ground here I knew you were in trouble. I could sense it in your heart, Jared. You're lonely and sad, and I am here to help you. That's why my meteor is gold."

Jared, while he was definitely confused, noticed the men in black's eyes go wide. He knew that if the government was about anything, it was definitely about money. He knew that those folks would kill for money, as they had obviously done before. He swallowed the fear in his belly before looking back at the alien.

"Well, what are you going to do about these guys? You and I both know they're not going to let us get out of here alive."

"I can't kill them," the alien shook his head.

Jared quickly threw his hands up. "I wasn't implying that!"

The alien smiled an almost playful smile. "I know. You're adorable when you're flustered."

Jared didn't know what to say to that.

"Can you wipe their memories or something?" Jared asked. "Or something like that?"

"I can, and that is what I planned to do," The alien smirked. "I'm not stupid, Jared."

"I didn't say you were!"

The alien snickered before flicking his hand. The men in black unfroze, seeming to become completely confused. They shook their heads and looked at Jared.

"I'm sorry sir, I can't seem to remember why we're here," he laughed at Jared.

"That's all right," Jared forced a wide smile on his face. "We get lots of travelers down this road. Maybe you missed the fork down the road that turns into the bigger town?"

The men nodded. "Yeah, probably. I'm so sorry to bug you, son. We'll be on our way."

They simply loaded into the cars that they came here in and drove away without another word. Jared looked at the alien and began to laugh in euphoria as the cars drove away.

"I can't believe you did that!" Jared cheered in a near childlike joy. "That's amazing!"

The alien winked at Jared. "If you let me come inside, I can show you all the other things I can do."

Jared blushed. "Okay...but I should warn you, there's a lot of glass on the floor."

Chapter 3

After changing into a borrowed pair of PJ's, the alien now sat at Jared's table. Jared was going to sweep all the glass into a pile and get it out of the way, but there was nothing that he could do once he walked in. True to his word, the alien had set everything back right. He even fixed the truck. Jared still wasn't sure that this wasn't some kind of fever dream that he was experiencing. Maybe he hit his head really hard when the meteor had come down, or worse: maybe he was really dead. Maybe he was in some kind of perfect purgatory, and this alien was actually an angel.

Jared made himself some coffee, and he made some for his new alien friend. He hoped that he would like coffee, but he would be surprised if the alien didn't. He was an alien, not a monster.

The alien sipped on the coffee as Jared finally sat down. The two of them stared out at Jared's land, watching the animals peacefully graze under the moonlight. For a moment, neither one said anything. It was peaceful, and quiet. Then, of course, Jared had to break it with his many, many questions.

"What is your name?" Jared asked.

The alien laughed. "That's your first real question?"

"Well, you know mine. I feel like it's only fair for me to know yours, right?"

The alien smiled and shrugged. "Well, I guess you're right. My real alien name isn't something I think you would be able to pronounce, I have to admit, but you can call me Katal."

Katal. What a beautiful name. Jared felt the name in his mouth, swirled it around like mouthwash. He wouldn't mind screaming that name in the bedroom, or whispering it to himself as they shared a bed.

"I know, it's weird," Katal laughed. "It doesn't sound American, does it?"

Jared gasped. "No, no! It's a beautiful name! Don't think that."

"I can think what I want, Jared of Earth," Katal smirked.

Damn, he was playful.

"So where do you come from?" Jared asked.

"I come from a planet in the next galaxy over," Katal explained. "We are a planet...well, I know this is cheesy, but we are a planet of built soulmates. We see lonely earthlings who don't have a match on this planet, because their match either passed away or was born somewhere on the other side of the world. We take their soul and put it inside one of us and come to Earth to help."

"So you're literally like a Build-A-Bear for soulmates?" Jared blinked.

"I don't know what that is," Katal shrugged, "but sure, sounds good."

Jared laughed. He found himself belly laughing for the first time in a long time, feeling elated. Maybe that explained their connection. They were soulmates, meant to be together. They were supposed to love one another with everything in them. Maybe that's why Jared couldn't stop thinking of him, or why he felt that he had a connection with the alien.

"So," Jared wrung his fingers together, "What do you know about me?"

"Let's see," Katal thought out loud. "I know your parents recently passed, God rest their souls. I know that you came out as a gay as a teenager, and I know that they were accepting. I know that you've only had one serious relationship that turned abusive, and I know that you've always wanted a cat but never seemed to get around to getting one. I know your favorite color is orange because you think it's a lonely color, your favorite food is chicken noodle soup, and your favorite sport is football."

Jared's eyes widened. "How the...what!? How did you know that!?"

Katal winked. "I did my research."

"Well, that's not fair!" Jared whined, feeling a hell of a lot like a child and not doing anything to fix that feeling. "I don't know anything about you, and you're supposed to be my soulmate! How am I supposed to be your soulmate if you don't tell me stuff about you?"

Katal laughed. "I never said I wasn't going to, did I? I'm going to tell you about myself as well, you silly head. You just have to give me a chance and stop whining."

Jared felt his entire face go hot. He swallowed and nodded, sitting back in his chair. He felt entirely stupid, but he didn't blame himself. He always got this way around attractive men that he liked. He pretended to find the window panes entirely interesting as Katal began to tell him about his life.

"I don't really know much about where I come from, exactly. I do know that we have a few people who are in charge, obviously, but like I said, we're a soulmate planet. We are simply vessels for the person that was meant for you. So, as far as I know, I was a shell of the man you were supposed to meet and fall in love with. Only thing was, when he was a child, he and his mother were hit by a drunk driver and they both passed on. I was supposed to come into your life subtly, but then I watched you more carefully and noticed how close you were to the edge, as nearly anyone would be of course. I didn't blame you. Your land was in jeopardy, your parents had passed, you were regretting everything you've ever done in your life. But, let me tell you something."

Katal looked into Jared's eyes steadily, smiling softly but not too widely. It was almost like he knew that what he was going to say was going to be a big deal and didn't want to say it, but knew he had too. Jared was on the edge of his seat, knowing all too well what was coming.

"I know part of you feels that maybe you should have gone to college, should have left them behind. Part of you feels like you missed out on something huge, but...Jared, the only important things in this world are experiences and loved ones. Sure, money is important, because it leads to a life that can be full of experiences and fun and amazing things to give your loved ones, but a life focused on dependability on money isn't a good one. You stayed when they needed you the most. You stayed and made memories with them. You gave your father peace of mind about his land, and you were there for your mother. I know you don't think she knew or even cared in those final days, but she knew that the bowls of soup on her dresser were from you. She knew that you were doing the laundry and the cleaning and the things she couldn't make herself do on her own. They loved you for staying, and they love you now. I can assure you that much. Don't regret staying for the people you love, ever."

Jared felt his stomach lurch. He was prepared for Katal to say something freaky, like "I have tentacles and we must use them in the bedroom," not this. Jared didn't know that he needed to hear it until he heard it, and it broke him.

He sobbed so suddenly, so loudly, that his whole body rocked with the momentum. He didn't know that his entire body had fallen from the chair until it did, his knees slapping against the wood floor hard. Katal was there, a stranger that knew him better than anyone else in the entire world. He held Jared in his strong arms, and he didn't say anything to him. He just pet his hair, gently, with rough hands. Jared wondered through his tears of grief what his father would have said about Katal's hands. He would have said something about Katal being a hard worker or some kind of laborer, and his mother would have laughed and said something about the possibility of Katal being an artist. They would have laughed and joked until Katal would break the silence by saying that he was actually a gymnast. The idea of his parents being here was enough to make him cry even harder, the sobs rocking his entire body. He hadn't cried like this in years, not since his father's cancer diagnosis. He hadn't cried like this because he didn't want to take attention away from his own mother's grief or his father's pain, and yet he didn't even take care of himself. Really, he knew he should have taken better care of himself, but he couldn't help it. He wasn't a selfish person, and there was nothing he could do to change that about himself.

Finally, when the tears ran dry and he was just hiccupping and wiping his nose on the back of his hands, Katal leaned against the wall and brought Jared into his lap. He didn't do anything other than cradle him like a baby, and yet, the action alone was enough to make Jared feel like a child again. The only thing he was missing was sucking on his thumb like a toddler. He closed his eyes and leaned against Katal's chest, resting his head on him fully. Katal rocked his body a little bit, soothing Jared's nerves as he hummed. Jared didn't even know what he was humming, he only knew that he loved it.

No one said anything, and no one needed to say anything. There was a silent understanding between the two men, and no one had to tell the other that they were feeling connected and warm. Jared didn't have to tell Katal that things between them were different now. Breaking down in front of someone like that changes things forever, no matter if you want them to or not.

Chapter 4

Jared couldn't remember when he stopped crying, or when Katal had carried him to his bed. He couldn't really remember much else other than waking up in his comfortable bed, in the clothes he was in the night before. It was uncomfortable, realizing that he slept in jeans, but at the same time he was happy that he was at least in clothes. Not that he would have minded Katal taking a peek or anything, but he would have much rather been awake for Katal's first time ever seeing him naked. It just made sense, at least to Jared.

"You're awake!" Katal called from the doorway.

He walked in with a cup of coffee in one hand and a plate of pancakes in the other. He set the plates down on the bedside table beside Jared before brushing his hair out of his eyes and smiling.

"Hey sleepyhead," Katal offered. "Did you have a peaceful sleep? I know it was a pretty intense night."

Jared nodded, yawning. His mouth felt sticky and gross from the night before, since he didn't brush his teeth. His throat was raw from crying.

"Well, that's good. I made your breakfast, and I'm going to go get you the orange juice I poured. Don't worry."

Jared didn't really see what he even needed to worry about at this point. Katal was taking care of everything, and Jared felt safe. He readjusted his pillow and leaned back, throwing his sweat stained shirt off in the corner of his room. He shrugged out of his jeans and tossed them in the corner of the room with the shirt before laying back down, automatically feeling ten times better. He had just readjusted when Katal walked in.

He was holding the orange juice that he promised, which didn't surprise Jared at all. He hadn't known Katal for long, sure, but he knew this alien well enough to know that when he said that he was going to do something, he was going to do it. However, what he didn't expect was the widening of Katal's eyes as he took in Jared's stature and size against the rest of the bed. Jared knew he looked good, so he leaned back with both his arms and put them under his arms and flexed his biceps. Katal's mouth kind of opened and kind of didn't, finding itself stuck in some kind of limbo of opening and not opening. He wasn't sure what he wanted to do, and Jared could tell.

"Like what you see?" Jared asked, wiggling under the covers.

Katal swallowed. "I...maybe..." Katal cleared his throat and shook his head, the red climbing on his cheeks.

Jared laughed. "I thought I was the flustered one here!"

"Well, you mafe me flustered just as well sir!" Katal pointed his finger at Jared in an accusing manner. "I didn't realize..."

"Didn't realize what?" Jared snickered. "How hot I am?"

Katal could only nod before setting his orange juice down on the counter. "I shouldn't be gawking at you. You had a terrible night, and you need to have your breakfast."

Jared got to his feet, slowly. He felt confident as he walked up to Katal, taking his pale, soft face in his hands. He ran his thumb along Katal's jawline before mumbling, "I am having my breakfast."

He kissed Katal.

It was better than any other kiss he had ever experienced in the entire world. Katal's lips were kind and caring, giving and soft in their own way. Katal inhaled breath, sharp and sudden, as Jared pressed his lips against him. His hands suddenly found their way into Jared's hair, and the sweet soft moment was gone.

Now there was a fierce need pulsing through Jared's veins. He kissed Katal harder, and the alien licked Jared's lips in a teasing fashion. Jared moaned, forcing Katal's mouth open and making their tongues dance. At this point, Katal was panting and moaning already, and the true play hadn't even begun yet.

Jared didn't hesitate. He grabbed Katal by the thighs and lifted him up, forcing Katal to wrap his legs around his waist before Katal slammed him into the wall. Katal cried out in pleasure as Jared buried his face in Katal's neck, sucking and licking it like a vampire in desperate need of blood. Katal's moans only spurred Jared on as he reached over and touched the penis he had been craving since the moment he saw it. When Katal screamed in elation just from Jared touching it, Jared knew it was time.

Jared gently carried Katal over to the bed, making him face the pillow. Katal got on his hind legs and waited, shaking with anticipation. Jared ran his hands along Katal's soft skin, sending sparks of electricity through Katal's body. Jared checked first with his fingers, spurred on by Katal's moans of pleasure.

"Are you sure?" Jared asked breathlessly.

Katal nodded. "Yes."

Jared pressed into him gently, and both men nearly screamed right there. The feeling was more than elation, it was pure bliss. Jared had to take a moment to breathe, trying to ensure that he didn't finish too early. God, he wanted to do anything but that. He wanted to take his time with Katal, he wanted to make sure that he gave him the best time of his life. Jared wanted to make him feel just as good as Jared felt.

Jared started slowly, and Katal started to moan even more. He begged for Jared to go faster, raising his hips in the air. Jared couldn't help it at that point. He was trying to go slow, but now, with Katal begging like that...he knew what he had to do.

He started ramming into Katal as hard as he could. Skin slapped against skin with loud claps, and Jared's legs trembled from the sensation. He cried out, moaning, and trying to make sure his legs didn't give out. Katal screamed that he was going to cum, and the next thing Jared knew, Katal's legs were flailing about and he was whimpering in pleasure, eyes rolled into the back of his head. It didn't take Jared very long to follow suit, nearly collapsing under the pressure of his own joy.

He finally pulled out, panting and nearly ready to fall over. Katal leaned against the bed, panting as well. Neither of them moved, but it wasn't because they chose not to. Neither of them really could after the feelings that were coursing through them. There was a moment of silence as they finally sighed and took a few steps. Both men were headed to the bathroom, stumbling and laughing with one another. They hopped in Jared's shower, but nothing sexy happened. They simply cleaned up, both afraid to even touch their happy places for fear of losing the feelings that were going through them. After a shower, they laid together in Jared's bed naked and holding each other. Katal rested his head on Jared's chest and inhaled the scent of him with each deep breath. Jared suddenly felt incredibly exhausted, and he knew he could fall asleep right then, but he didn't. Instead, he listened to Katal's breathing. He listened to the way he inhaled and held it, listening to the air in his lungs before he pushed it out again. Jared smiled, and for the first time in what felt like forever, he felt truly and genuinely content.

"It is real gold on my ship," Katal whispered.

"Mmm?" Was all Jared could ask, continuing to run his hands through Katal's mop of hair on the top of his head.

"My ship has real gold on it," Katal nodded. "It can save your land, I promise. That's why I brought it. It can help you make those payments!"

Jared smiled even wider, his eyes still closed. "That's amazing, Katal. Thank you. That's very thoughtful of you."

"Of course," He smiled and snuggled into Jared's chest. "I only wanted to bring you happiness and joy, and I knew I could do that with the meteor. That way at least you would be more happy and not worrying about those payments!"

Jared sighed and kissed the top of Katal's head. It was a sweet gesture, and it took Katal by surprise. Sure, they just had mind-blowing sex, but the kindness in the gesture felt like something more. Like they were actually a couple, actually together. This is a question that Jared hadn't formally asked Katal yet, and he didn't want to make assumptions. Sure, he was supposed to be his soulmate, and they were supposed to be together, but Jared hadn't asked him. Just because they had sex didn't mean that they had to be together forever, no matter how much Jared wanted it. It was only fair if they did get together, however, so Jared started thinking of a plan to ask Katal out in a sweet way that he would like, only to realize that he had no idea what Katal actually liked.

"What are you thinking about?" Katal asked as Jared stared at the wall.

"Well," Jared admitted, "I was thinking about the things you liked. You never told me the things that you liked, you know."

Katal laughed before poking Jared on the nose. "I like you."

Jared snickered. "Other than me, Katal."

"Well," Katal tried to think. "I do like sports, and apparently I love the outdoors and hiking, as well as kayaking. My favorite food is Chinese food, supposedly, though I've never had it. My favorite color is green because it reminds me of vegetation which your planet is losing a little fast for my liking, you know?"

Jared nodded. "Yeah, no, I get it. That's exactly how I feel."

Katal nodded, leaning farther into Jared's chest. "So, is that what you wanted to know?"

Jared smiled. "Yes, I think that's perfect."

Jared was formulating a perfect plan in his head. Before he could execute this plan, however, he knew he needed to get Katal's help with the rest of it.

"Okay," Jared started. "I need your help with this, and then we'll go on the best date of your life."

"I've never been on a date," Katal whispered.

"Well, then, I won't have much competition," Jared laughed before slowly getting up.

He was still reeling from that sex session as he slowly pulled on his clothes and jeans, making his way toward the bed. He had some clothes folded up that he was sure would fit Katal. He was about to offer it to him when he saw that the alien had tried to put the pillowcase on as a top.

Jared died laughing despite Katal's pleas for help.

"Why were you going to wear a pillowcase to our date?"

"I thought this was a shirt," Katal pouted. "I'm sorry."

"Don't be sorry," Jared shook his head. "That was hilarious and I'm really glad that you did it. I needed that laugh."

Katal smiled. "Well, in that case, I'm glad I thought pillow cases were what humans wore."

Jared couldn't stifle his smile as he walked toward Katal, handing him the clothes he could change into. Katal put on one of Jared's old flannels and Levi jeans, then threw a jacket on over it. When he turned to look at Jared, eyes wide and earnest like a puppy, Jared couldn't help it.

He pulled Katal in for a hug and kissed him on the forehead, not caring what the gesture meant. "You look handsome."

The two of them walked outside toward the meteor. It still sat there, undisturbed, but Jared knew better. His neighbors would want to know what a giant, gold rock was doing on the property soon. That is, if the neighbors got to it before the government got mad and decided to come back. They needed to move it before someone saw it and tried to steal it, or worse.

"How am I supposed to get this to the bank?" Katal asked, innocently looking at Jared with the widest eyes he had ever seen.

Jared was about to make a joke about how innocent he was, about to say something about the fact that banks don't take giant rocks of gold for payment, when Jared realized he had no idea where to take the gold rock either.

Where was he supposed to go to get the best value for that rock?

"I don't even know where I need to take this," Jared admitted.

Katal snickered. "What, do you think I know where to take it?"

Jared whipped out his phone and pulled up Google. He was about to hit the search button when a couple familiar trucks rumbled down the road. Jared's blood ran cold, and Katal seemed to notice. Katal narrowed his eyes as five men climbed out of the trucks. Jared noticed the guns strapped to their hips immediately, and the burrs on their boots clinked loudly with each step. They snickered when they saw Jared and Katal.

"Well, look who it is," The first guy snickered. "It's the little pee-pee lover of the town."

Jared tensed.

Sure, he hadn't experienced any homophobia from his parents, but he would be stupid to expect to not expect it from anywhere else. That, of course, came from the men that worked with Jared's father. Full grown men who thought that the best way to make Jared "un-gay" was to show him what it took to be a man. There was talk of getting him to conversion therapy, or making him sleep with another gay woman church, which was a horrifying experience all together. Jared's father was having none of that of course. His father had made a threat to all of the men that if they stepped foot on his land they would be shot. Jared now thought about his gun, propped against the door, which he didn't feel the need to grab. The main leader of the group, Todd, had a piece of hay in his mouth. He chuckled and leaned against his car door.

"My, oh my, is that a little boyfriend that I see?"

Jared's voice felt trapped. He didn't know what to say But he certainly wanted to say something. However, every time that he looked at these men, he felt like he was a teenager again in the barn with those men after they paid their son to pretend to like Jared, only to get him to come to the barn. There, they had beat him bloody. They had called him slurs. Now, even as a full grown man, and after such mind-blowing sex with Katal, Jared felt his legs tremble underneath him.

"Yes," Katal stated boldly. "What is it to you, huh?" He demanded.

Todd whistled, hooting and hollering with his friends. "Looks like this pixie has some bark to his bite."

Katal narrowed his eyes. "I'm not a pixie. You're just insecure."

Jared reached out and took Katal's hand, squeezing.

Katal squeezed back. Jared was sure that he could see the expression of fear on his face. Katal didn't act like he could, though. He couldn't take his eyes off of the men leaning against the cars. He wouldn't let himself look away.

"You heard me," Katal reminded the men quite loudly. "You're insecure because you find yourself getting hard at gay porn, don't you big boy?"

Todd dropped his hay. His mouth fell open. He took a few staggered steps back.

"How dare you!?" he screamed at him.

"Your wife knows too, Todd," Katal smirked devilishly at the poor excuse of the man. "That's why she has to use the vibrator every time that you have sex."

Todd was too shocked to react, and frankly, so was Jared. He was too busy trying not to laugh as Katal continued through the rest of Todd's cronies.

"Terry, you're too scared to stand up against them and tell your friends that you're actually an ally because your sister is gay too. Andy, you're here just for the gold rock on the land, which you aren't going to get. And frankly, Hank and Connor, you're just...your heads are empty, so I really don't know why you're here other than to have someone lead you, even if it's too the gates of Hell."

Hank and Connor just giggled as if something was funny.

"Enough of this!" Todd screamed, stomping his boot on the dirt road. "Give us that rock, or we'll kill you two. We were just going to beat you to a bloody pulp, like we used too," Todd smiled at Jared then, "But now, you've crossed a line. You're dead."

Katal shook his head. "See, I don't think that's true. I think you're all going to climb back into your trucks and forget that any of this happened. I also think that Todd, after you run your car into the pole outside your home, and survive of course, I just want you to total your car; you're going to come clean to your wife and the town. You're also going to accidentally run into your father, and I'll let that play out as it is. Now," Katal flicked his hand and sparks flew from his fingertips. "Go now. I don't want to be kept waiting."

Miraculously, all of Jared's childhood bullies climbed in their trucks just like the government had and drove away without a question. They drove off into the sunset and acted like they hadn't even shown up in the first place.

"How did you do that!?" Jared cried, cheerful.

"I can't tell you," Katal kissed Jared's cheek. "Let's just say that my kind know a bully when we see one, and we are the bringers of cosmic justice."

Jared didn't drop Katal's hand as they stared at their land, their future together, once Jared asked Katal to officially be his boyfriend of course. Finally, Jared squeezed Katal's hand.

"So, about that rock..."

THE END